STAR WARS
REBELS™

MEET THE
REBELS

Written by Sadie Smith

LONDON, NEW YORK, MUNICH,
MELBOURNE AND DELHI

DK LONDON
Senior Editor Sadie Smith
Pre-Production Producer Siu Yin Chan
Producer David Appleyard
Managing Editor Laura Gilbert
Managing Art Editor Maxine Pedliham
Art Director Lisa Lanzarini
Publishing Manager Julie Ferris
Publishing Director Simon Beecroft

DK DELHI
Editor Rahul Ganguly
Art Editor Suzena Sengupta
Managing Editor Chitra Subramanyam
Managing Art Editor Neha Ahuja
Pre-Production Manager Sunil Sharma
DTP Designers Rajdeep Singh, Umesh Singh Rawat

For Lucasfilm
Executive Editor Jonathan W. Rinzler
Art Director Troy Alders
Keeper of the Holocron Leland Chee
Director of Publishing Carol Roeder

Reading Consultant
Maureen Fernandes

First published in 2014 in Great Britain by
Dorling Kindersley Limited
80 Strand, London, WC2R 0RL

10 9 8 7 6 5 4 3 2 1
001–195511–Aug/14

A CIP catalogue record for this book is available from the British Library.

ISBN: 978-1-40935-724-7

Colour reproduction by Alta Image Ltd, UK
Printed and bound in China by South China Printing Company Ltd.

Discover more at
www.dk.com
www.starwars.com

Contents

4 Rebellion on Lothal

6 Planet Lothal

8 Ezra Bridger

10 Special Power

12 What is the Force?

14 Kanan Jarrus

16 Garazeb "Zeb" Orrelios

18 Find the Rebels!

20 Hera Syndulla

22 The *Ghost*

24 Sabine Wren

26 Rebel Weapons

28 C1-10P "Chopper"

30 Chopper and Ezra

32 Rebels: Fact Files

34 Aresko and Grint

36 Agent Kallus

38 The Inquisitor

40 Rebel Battle Tips

42 Quiz

44 Glossary

45 Index

46 Guide for Parents

Rebellion on Lothal

Meet the rebels.
Their names are
Sabine, Ezra, Kanan,
Hera, Zeb and Chopper.
They live on a planet
called Lothal.

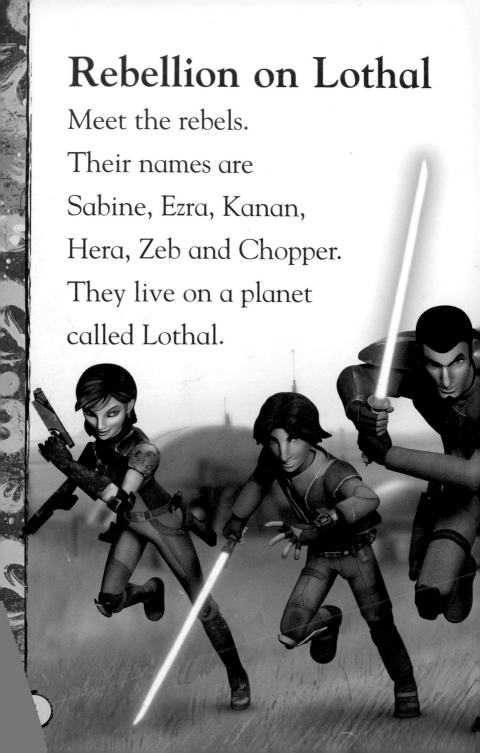

Lothal is under the rule
of an evil Empire.
The rebels are fighting
against the Empire
and its soldiers.

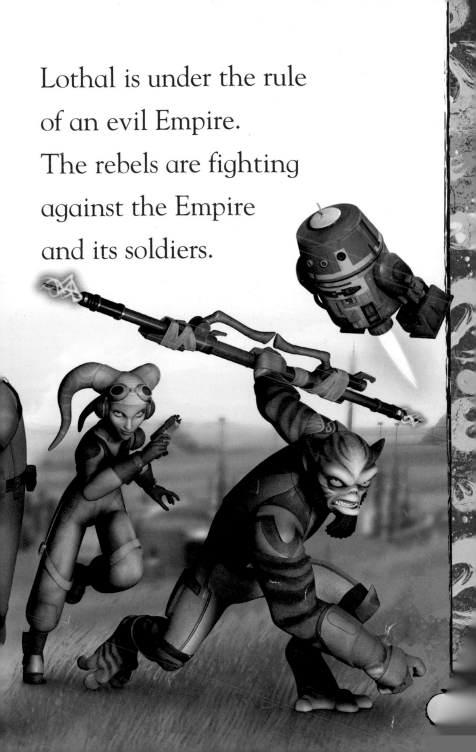

PLANET LOTHAL

Long roads with tunnels join other towns on Lothal to the capital city.

The factories of the Empire blow out thick, black smoke. This makes it difficult to breathe in the city.

The capital city is full of tall, white buildings. Only rich people who work for the Empire can live in them.

Farm buildings in the grasslands may be hiding rebels.

Ezra Bridger

This is Ezra.

He is just 14 years old, but
he is brave and smart.

Ezra is also a lot of fun!

He likes to play jokes and
steal helmets from
the Emperor's soldiers.

Special Power

Ezra is special.

Sometimes, he can see
things a few seconds
before they happen.
This is because Ezra is
in touch with a special power
called the Force.

Ezra does not understand
how to use this power.

Maybe someone
can teach him...

WHAT IS THE FORCE?

The Force is a mysterious energy
that flows through all living creatures.
A few special people, such as Ezra,
can use the Force to do amazing things...

FORCE FACT
Learning to use
the Force is not easy.
Ezra will learn that
it takes years
to become
an expert.

FORCE FACT
Knowing how to
use the Force can
make a person wise
and powerful.
But it can also
turn them evil.

Ezra can move things
without touching them.

The Force helps Ezra to see things before they actually happen.

FORCE FACT
A group called the Jedi can use the Force. Ezra knows one of the Jedi.

Without the Force, a lightsaber is very difficult to use well.

Kanan Jarrus

Kanan is a Jedi.
The Jedi are trained
to fight for good.
Their job is to protect
the galaxy from evil.
The Emperor does
not like the Jedi,
so Kanan has to keep
his Jedi skills secret.

Garazeb "Zeb" Orrelios

The rebel Zeb is
very big and strong.
He is a Lasat from
the planet Lasan.
Zeb likes nothing better
than to fight stormtroopers.
The stormtroopers are
soldiers in the army of
the evil Emperor.

PROTECT THE EMPIRE
FIND THE REBELS!

Help the Empire defeat rebellion!
Report any rebels to your nearest
stormtrooper base on Lothal.

THE EMPIRE NEEDS YOU!

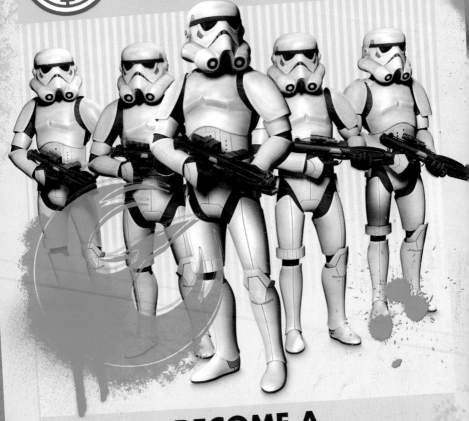

BECOME A STORMTROOPER!
Help keep the peace on Lothal.
Uniforms and weapons provided to all recruits.

Hera Syndulla

Hera is a Twi'lek from
a planet called Ryloth.
This clever rebel leads
the group with Kanan.
She plans all their missions.
Hera owns a spaceship
called the *Ghost*.
She is a great pilot.

THE GHOST

Bubble-shaped
cockpit

Forward gun turret
under cockpit

Diamond-shaped body

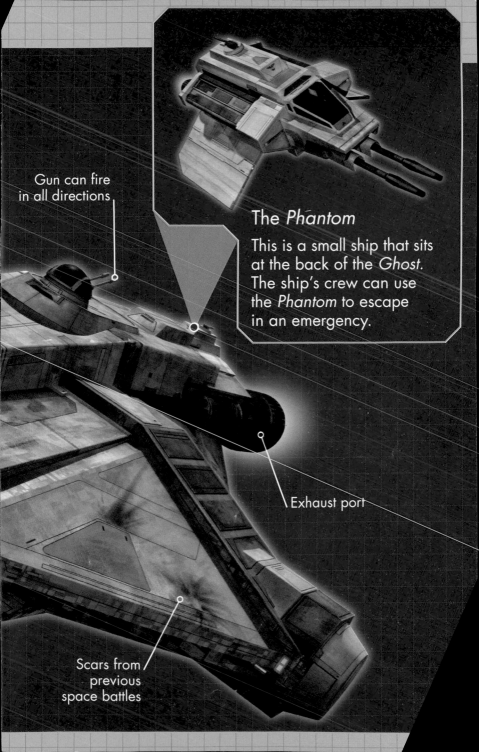

Gun can fire
in all directions

The *Phantom*

This is a small ship that sits
at the back of the *Ghost*.
The ship's crew can use
the *Phantom* to escape
in an emergency.

Exhaust port

Scars from
previous
space battles

Sabine Wren

Colourful Sabine
is an artist from the
planet Mandalore.
She is usually covered
in paint!
Sabine looks after the
weapons of the rebels.
She is also good at
blowing things up.

REBEL
WEAPONS

Ezra's slingshot

The slingshot is attached neatly to the wrist. It fires balls of energy at the enemy.

Energy slingshot

Sabine's twin blasters

Blaster

Two blasters mean two chances to hit the target! Blasters shoot bursts of energy called bolts.

Kanan's lightsaber

The lightsaber is a
very special weapon.
It is a bit like a sword,
but has a blade made
of pure energy.

Lightsaber

Zeb's Bo-rifle

Zappers at both ends of
Zeb's bo-rifle can stun
anyone who gets in his way.
It doubles up as a battle
staff to whack enemies.

Bo-rifle

Hera's boot-holstered blaster

Hera likes to keep her small,
powerful blaster close.
It is kept in a special
holster in her boot.

Boot holster

C1-10P "Chopper"

Chopper is a type of robot
called an astromech droid.
He helps the rebels
by repairing their spaceship.
Chopper speaks a
special robot language.
Only Hera and Sabine
can understand him.

Chopper and Ezra

Most of the rebels think
Chopper is too grumpy.
They do not even try to
be friends with him.
However, Ezra loves
playing jokes on Chopper.
The little droid likes to
play jokes on Ezra, too!

REBELS

Ezra Bridger

Species: Human, from the planet Lothal

Age: 14 (almost 15!)

Special skills: Feeling the Force

Kanan Jarrus

Species: Human, from the planet Coruscant

Age: 27

Special skills: Jedi powers, leading battles

Hera Syndulla

Species: Twi'lek, from the planet Ryloth

Age: 24

Special skills: Ace pilot, sharp shooter

Sabine Wren

Species: Human, from the planet Mandalore

Age: 16

Special skills: Artistic, bomb expert, fixing gadgets and weapons

Garazeb "Zeb" Orrelios

Species: Lasat, from the planet Lasan

Age: Unknown

Special skills: Very strong, has lots of energy

C1-10P "Chopper"

Species: Astromech droid

Age: Unknown (but very old!)

Special skills: Repairing starships, understanding computers, playing jokes

Aresko and Grint

Aresko and Grint are
bad guys who work
for the evil Empire.
Aresko is pale and thin.
He thinks he is very
clever – but he is not!
Grint is tall and bulky.
He is just a big bully.

Agent Kallus

Agent Kallus works for
the Empire's secret police.
This villain tracks people
who are plotting against
the Emperor.

Agent Kallus is clever
and dangerous.

Watch out, rebels!

The Inquisitor

This scary villain carries
a powerful lightsaber
with two blades!
The Inquisitor has
been sent to Lothal
by Agent Kallus.
His job is to hunt
for Jedi who may be
hiding on the planet.

KANAN'S BATTLE TIPS

"Learn the ways of the Force. With the Force, you can throw enemies out of the way."

"Plan your battles well and make decisions quickly!"

"Practice your lightsaber skills. The Inquisitor has a double-ended lightsaber. He is hard to beat in a duel."

ZEB'S BATTLE TIPS

Try the one-swing knockout. It can take out two stormtroopers with one blow!

Use the bo-rifle's zapper. The powerful beam can stun even the strongest enemy.

If you are a big guy like me, use the full force of your weight to knock your enemies over!

Quiz

1. Which planet do the rebels live on?

2. What is Ezra's special power called?

3. What is the favourite weapon of the Jedi?

4. Who does the *Ghost* spaceship belong to?

5. What does Kanan have to keep secret?

6. Which planet is
   Sabine from?

7. Who does Zeb like
   to fight?

8. What type of robot
   is Chopper?

9. Who does Agent Kallus
   work for?

10. What weapon does
    the Inquisitor use?

Answers on
page 45

Glossary

Emperor
Somebody who rules over a group of nations

Gadget
A small device or a machine made
for a special purpose

Holster
A case for carrying a blaster gun

Lightsaber
A swordlike weapon with
a blade of pure energy

Pilot
A person who flies a spacecraft

Species
A kind or type of being, such
as human

The Force
The energy created by all living things

Index

Agent Kallus 37, 38

Aresko 35

astromech droid 29, 33

blaster 26–27

bo-rifle 27, 41

Chopper 4, 29, 30, 33

Coruscant 32

Emperor 4, 5, 8, 14, 16, 18, 37

Ezra 4, 8, 10, 12, 13, 26, 30, 32

Force 10, 12–13, 32, 40

Ghost, the 20, 22–23

Grint 35

Hera 4, 20, 27, 29, 32

Inquisitor, the 38, 40

Jedi 13, 14, 32, 38

Kanan 4, 14, 27, 32, 40

Lasan 16, 33

Lasat 16, 33

lightsaber 13, 27, 38, 40

Lothal 4, 6–7, 18, 19, 32, 38

Mandalore 25, 33

Phantom, the 23

rebel 4–5, 7, 16, 18, 20, 25, 26, 29, 30, 32, 37

Ryloth 20, 32

Sabine 4, 25, 26, 29, 33

slingshot 26

stormtroopers 16, 18–19

taser 27, 41

Twi'lek 20, 32

Zeb 4, 16, 27, 33, 41

Answers to the quiz on pages 42 and 43:
1. Lothal 2. The Force 3. A lightsaber 4. Hera
5. His Jedi skills 6. Mandalore 7. Stormtroopers
8. Astromech droid 9. The Secret Police
10. A lightsaber with two blades

Guide for Parents

DK Reads is a three-level reading series for children, developing the habit of reading widely for both pleasure and information. These books have exciting running text interspersed with a range of reading genres to suit your child's reading ability, as required by the school curriculum. Each book is designed to develop your child's reading skills, fluency, grammar awareness and comprehension in order to build confidence and engagement when reading.

Ready for a *Beginning to Read* book
YOUR CHILD SHOULD

- be using phonics, including combinations of consonants, such as bl, gl and sm, to read unfamiliar words; and common word endings, such as plurals, ing, ed and ly.

- be using the storyline, illustrations and the grammar of a sentence to check and correct their own reading.

- be pausing briefly at commas, and for longer at full stops; and altering his/her expression to respond to question, exclamation and speech marks.

A Valuable And Shared Reading Experience

For many children, reading requires much effort but adult participation can make this both fun and easier. So here are a few tips on how to use this book with your child.

TIP 1: Check out the contents together before your child begins:

- Read the text about the book on the back cover.
- Read through and discuss the contents page together to heighten your child's interest and expectation.
- Briefly discuss any unfamiliar or difficult words on the contents page.

- Chat about the non-fiction reading features used in the book, such as headings, captions, recipes, lists or charts.

This introduction helps to put your child in control and makes the reading challenge less daunting.

TIP 2: Support your child as he/she reads the story pages:

- Give the book to your child to read and turn the pages.
- Where necessary, encourage your child to break a word into syllables, sound out each one and then flow the syllables together. Ask him/her to reread the sentence to check the meaning.
- When there's a question mark or an exclamation mark, encourage your child to vary his/her voice as he/she reads the sentence. Demonstrate how to do this if it is helpful.

TIP 3: Praise, share and chat:

- The factual pages tend to be more difficult than the story pages, and are designed to be shared with your child.
- Ask questions about the text and the meaning of the words used. Ask your child to suggest his/her own quiz questions. These help to develop comprehension skills and awareness of the language used.

A FEW ADDITIONAL TIPS

- Try and read together every day. Little and often is best. After 10 minutes, only keep going if your child wants to read on.
- Always encourage your child to have a go at reading difficult words by themselves. Praise any self-corrections, for example, "I like the way you sounded out that word and then changed the way you said it, to make sense."
- Read other books of different types to your child just for enjoyment and information.

Here are some other DK Reads you might enjoy.

Beginning to Read

Pirate Attack!
Come and join Captain Blackbeard and his pirate crew for
an action-packed adventure on the high seas.

Deadly Dinosaurs
Roar! Thud! Meet Roxy, Sid, Deano and Sonia, the museum
dinosaurs that come alive at night.

LEGO® Legends of Chima™: Tribes of Chima
Enter the mysterious land of Chima™ and discover
the amazing animal tribes who live there.

Starting to Read Alone

Battle at the Castle
Through the letters of a squire to his sister, discover life in
a medieval castle during peacetime and war.

African Adventures
Experience the trip of a lifetime on an
African safari as recorded in Katie's diary.
Share her excitement when seeing wild animals up close.

LEGO® Legends of Chima™: Heroes' Quest
Who are the mysterious Legend Beasts? Join the heroes of Chima™
on their quest to find these mythical creatures.